June Crebbin was a primary school teacher before taking early retirement to concentrate on her writing. She is the author of a number of books for children, including the first three stories about Merryfield Hall Riding School, *Jumping Beany*, *Saving Oscar* and *Riding High*, as well as several picture books for younger children. June lives in Leicestershire, where she enjoys riding in the countryside and in the dressage arena.

More books about
Merryfield Hall Riding School

*Jumping Beany*
*Saving Oscar*
*Riding High*

More books by the same author

*The Curse of the Skull*
*The Dragon Test*
*Emmelina and the Monster*
*Hal the Highwayman*
*Horse Tales*
*No Tights for George!*
*Tarquin the Wonder Horse*

# Stealing Emerald

**June Crebbin**

This is a work of fiction. Names, characters, places and incidents are either the product of the author's imagination or, if real, are used fictitiously. All statements, activities, stunts, descriptions, information and material of any other kind contained herein are included for entertainment purposes only and should not be relied on for accuracy or replicated as they may result in injury.

First published 2009 by Walker Books Ltd
87 Vauxhall Walk, London SE11 5HJ

2 4 6 8 10 9 7 5 3 1



This book has been typeset in Stempel Schneidler

Printed and bound in Great Britain by
Clays Ltd, St Ives plc



British Library Cataloguing in Publication Data:
a catalogue record for this book
is available from the British Library

ISBN 978-1-4063-1703-9

www.walker.co.uk

*For Catherine Holden*

*With special thanks to Gail*
*of Somerby Equestrian Centre; and to*
*Sue and Pam of Stapleford Park*

Early one morning, Amber was in the wash-box at Merryfield Hall Riding School, soaping her pony, Oscar's, tail, when her best friend, Molly, burst in with some news.

"Princess who?" Amber asked, looking up.

Molly was pleased to have grabbed Amber's attention.

"I don't know her name," she said. "But she's coming here! From somewhere far away, like..." She tried fervently to remember the conversation she had overheard between Jen, the owner of the riding school, and Carol, who worked in the office. "The Middle East!" she said triumphantly. "And," she carried on quickly as Amber turned back to rubbing the soap into Oscar's tail, "she's coming TODAY!"

Amber was still listening. "But why? Don't princesses usually open or inspect things? We're not doing anything special, are we?"

"No," Molly had to admit. "Not that I've heard."

Amber emptied the bucket of soapy water and refilled it with fresh.

"Aren't you excited?" cried Molly. "I wonder what she'll be like?"

"Probably be wearing a tiara," said Amber, dipping Oscar's tail in and out of the clean water and squeezing the soap out as she did so.

"Oh!" gasped Molly. "Do you think so?"

Amber grinned. "And a ball-gown. Maybe glass slippers?"

"Now you're being silly," said Molly. "Though if I had a tiara, I'd wear it every single day."

"It wouldn't exactly fit under your riding hat!" said Amber. She checked her watch. "You'd better fetch Feather," she advised. "Five minutes until our lesson."

Amber took Oscar back to his stable and tacked him up. He looked lovely. His chestnut coat shone, and his mane and tail were creamy white once again.

It was the first day of the summer holidays. Amber planned to spend all day every day at the stables from now on. She loved working there, and the free lessons she received for doing so – together with her usual weekly one – would be a big help in achieving her ambition. This year she was old enough to take part in the One-Day Event that would be held as part of the summer show in the grounds of Merryfield Hall Hotel. As always, Amber wanted to win, but the competition involved jumping, cross-country and dressage. The first two Amber had been doing for a while, but dressage was new to her and she was finding it difficult.

Amber arrived at the indoor arena as Molly appeared with Feather.

"Any sign?" said Molly as they mounted.

"Of what?" said Amber.

"The princess, of course," hissed Molly.

Amber gazed around. "Can't see a golden coach and six white horses," she murmured.

Molly rolled her eyes. She kicked Feather forward. Amber followed. Kate was instructing them.

"Move your ponies on," she said. "Get them stepping underneath you."

Amber settled into her saddle. When they'd first been told about dressage, she'd thought it sounded boring. Anyway, all the riders in her group – Lydia, Jack, Donna and Molly – knew how to make their ponies walk, trot and canter. But then, as they'd begun to have lessons, she'd realized there was a lot more to it than that. Dressage was about *how* you did those things; trying to achieve the same quality of movement in the arena that your pony used when he was free in the fields.

"Sit tall in the saddle," said Kate. "But deep so that your legs fall towards the ground. That's good, Lydia. Well done."

Lydia looks so relaxed, thought Amber. She envied the way Lydia could stretch her body upwards and her legs downwards, apparently so easily. Amber felt she was straining every nerve to obtain the correct position – and that only created tension.

The arena was marked out with letters. In the show, the rider had to complete a series of movements – making transitions exactly at the markers, not before, not after – and keep a consistent rhythm, neither hurrying nor dawdling. It was so difficult to get everything right.

"Let's begin at the beginning," said Kate. "One at a time. Enter at Marker A at a working trot and continue down the centre line to Marker C."

There wasn't really a line from A to C. You had to imagine it, and as the dressage judge would be positioned at C, it was important to make a good first impression.

Lydia started on Silver. "Plan your turn," called Kate. But Lydia misjudged it and went way past the marker. Jack did well on Roger to begin with, then wobbled towards C. Donna on Sparkle completed the whole manoeuvre without a hitch. "Excellent!" said Kate. Donna smirked.

"Oh, it's me," said Molly. She urged Feather forwards.

"A little slow," said Kate when Molly eventually reached C. "But accurate. Amber, off you go."

Oscar leapt forward. Amber tried to hold him back a little as they swung into the turn at A, but Oscar slowed almost to a walk. Quickly, Amber urged him on. Oscar responded, flew down the centre line, rounded the turn at C at speed, then stopped so abruptly that Amber fell forwards onto his neck. She heard the others laugh as she wriggled back into the saddle.

"Don't worry," said Kate. "Once Oscar settles to an even rhythm, he'll be fine."

Next it was the Serpentine. You had to ride the whole length of the arena, crossing from side to side in three equal loops.

"Follow my leader," said Kate. Which worked well until Amber caught up and had to slow down. She and Molly ended up muddled together.

"That's not fair!" shouted Amber.

"I couldn't help it," said Molly.

Donna laughed.

"Never mind," said Kate. "We'll do it again and you can go first, Amber. Then we'll do some canter work."

At the end of the lesson, Amber put Oscar away and fetched one of the large brooms to sweep the yard. Her loops in the Serpentine had been anything but equal, she reflected. She'd concentrated so hard on shape. The first one had turned out well but was far too big while the remaining two had become smaller and smaller. Amber knew she needed to have good shapes *and* size. It was no use having one without the other.

As she swept closer to the office, the door opened and Jen came out accompanied by a girl of about Amber's age.

"Ah, Amber," said Jen. "Just the person! Come and meet—"

She was cut short by an ear-splitting shout: "LOOSE HORSE!"

"Shut the gate!" yelled Jen, running to do it herself.

A large bay horse trotted briskly into the yard.

"It's Solomon," Amber told the girl. "He's

always getting out. If someone forgets to shut the bolt at the bottom of his stable door, he undoes the top one with his teeth. He likes to go for a wander."

"Couldn't that be dangerous?" said the girl, seriously. "And very careless of his groom."

Amber stared at her. "Jen'll be back in a minute," she said. Who did this girl think she was with her airs and graces?

The girl held out her hand. "It's very nice to meet you," she said. "I'm Princess Rana. And you are...?"

"Did you curtsy?" said Molly, when she met Amber for lunch in the field behind the stables.

"I did not," said Amber.

"I'm sure I would have done," said Molly. "After all, she is a princess."

Amber shrugged.

"What happened then?" asked Molly. "Where is she now?"

"With Jen," said Amber. She frowned. It was a relief telling Molly all about it. The morning hadn't been a huge success. After Solomon had been safely returned to his stable, Jen had asked Amber to show

Princess Rana around. Usually, Amber had no problem being friendly, and "a guest is a guest and worthy of respect", as Mum was so fond of telling her. But the princess had found fault with everything. First, the stables were too small. Some of the horses, apparently, could hardly turn around; then the tack room was overcrowded, the office a mess, and the kitchen tiny. Not one good word about anything.

At last, with all the politeness she could manage, Amber had said, "I suppose you're used to much grander things."

"Of course," the princess had replied, and as Amber was certainly not going to give her the satisfaction of boasting about that grandeur, she had pressed for no further details.

"Well, I would have," said Molly. "I'm only sorry I had to go to the dentist and miss it all. Anyway, did you at least discover what she's doing here?"

Amber jumped to her feet. "I think we're

about to find out," she said. "Get your curtsy ready."

Walking across the grass towards them were Jen and the princess. Molly scrambled up. "What do we call her?" she hissed.

"Don't tempt me," muttered Amber.

Molly soon had all the information she desired. Rana, as the princess was to be known, would be staying at Merryfield Hall Hotel until the end of the holidays; she would be coming to the riding school every day and helping out generally. Amber and Molly exchanged glances. A princess working at a stables?

"Just like you two," said Jen. "Now, what's on your list for today?"

"Tack-cleaning's next," said Amber.

"We usually do it outside," said Molly, "when the weather's fine."

Jen nodded. She turned to the princess. "Amber and Molly will look after you. They're two of my best helpers."

Amber's heart sank. The afternoon stretched ahead. She doubted very much that Rana had ever cleaned tack in her life. Even Donna, who kept her pony, Sparkle, at Merryfield Hall Livery Yard, boasted that someone did it for her – and her parents were only rich, not super-rich, as Rana's must be.

There was an awkward silence as Jen departed. On the way to the tack room, Amber said, "Have you done this before, Rana?"

"No," Rana replied.

"Oh, you'll love it," said Molly.

Amber tried not to giggle. Since when had Molly *enjoyed* tack-cleaning? Though it was pleasant enough when you could do it in the sunshine with just your best friend for company. Jen never minded all the chatting that went on as long as they were working.

Rana had plenty to say about tack-cleaning. No sooner had they started than she expressed disgust at the state of the cloths they were using, the fiddliness of the straps she was expected to undo and the amount of *dirt* on everything...

Amber couldn't stop herself. "But that's why we're cleaning it," she said. "That's the whole point."

"You're doing really well," Molly told Rana. She explained how important it was to keep the leather in good condition. "It needs attention every week at least," she said.

Rana looked horrified.

"Tack should be cleaned every time you ride your pony," said Amber.

"Which pony will you be riding?" asked Molly.

"I've no idea," said Rana abruptly. She turned away quickly, but not before Amber had seen the startled expression that flitted across her face.

"Oh well, it doesn't matter," said Molly kindly. "I'm sure Jen will give you a nice one."

Rana made a great business of rinsing and wringing out her cloth. She didn't look up.

Just then, a car drove in and stopped. Out stepped Donna – a vision in lilac jodhpurs, lilac chaps and an aqua and lilac T-shirt. She came towards them.

Amber braced herself. As if they hadn't enough to cope with!

"Hiya!" Donna called. Amber grunted a reply. Molly said hello. Rana said nothing.

"I've come to help," Donna announced.

Amber nearly exploded. Donna, *help*? She'd never lifted a finger before. She simply arrived with darling Sparkle for her lesson and departed at the end. That was it.

"Why?" said Amber, knowing perfectly well.

"Jen gave me permission," replied Donna. "She said she can always use an extra pair of hands." She spread her hands out in front of her as she spoke and looked at them doubtfully. The fingernails were perfectly manicured and painted the palest shade of pearly lilac.

"Oh!" gasped Molly. "Do you think you should? You'll ruin them!"

"I don't mind," said Donna bravely. She looked pointedly in Rana's direction. "Introduce me," she hissed.

"This is Princess Rana," said Molly obediently.

Donna moved towards the princess. "It's nice to meet you," she said and then performed a deep curtsy. Amber could scarcely take it in. The annoying thing was, Donna did it so gracefully, even in her jodhpurs.

Rana smiled. "Please. There's no need."

"But there is," insisted Donna, sickening sweetness dripping off every syllable. "You're a princess." She picked up a cloth. "Now, let me help you with that."

The gesture was somewhat of an empty one, as Donna had no idea what to do with the cloth. Molly dashed to the rescue, handing Donna a bridle and showing her how to wash all the straps first and then apply the saddle soap. “Rub it in well,” she advised.

Actually, thought Amber as the afternoon wore on, it was quite useful having Donna there. As always, she rabbited on about the fabulous feats of fearless Sparkle, but now she had a new audience. Not that there was much in the way of response from Rana.

Eventually Donna stopped talking about herself long enough to ask the princess a question. “Do you ride a lot?” she enquired. Donna hardly seemed to notice that this was met with complete silence. “I ride every day,” she continued. “Sometimes twice. Are your parents a king and queen? I suppose they must be. But they could be a duke and duchess...” She paused. There was still no response from Rana. She simply carried on applying soap to the saddle she was working on as if Donna hadn’t spoken.

"Do you live in a palace?" Donna went on. "I expect you do. What's it like?"

Still no answer. Amber wondered why Donna didn't just leave it. It was obvious Rana didn't want to talk about her home and family.

But Donna wasn't known for her sensitivity. "I don't suppose you've brought your precious jewel with you, have you?" she said next. "Your priceless emerald?"

At that, Rana turned, her face hot and angry. "What do you know about my Emerald?" she blazed. "Who told you?"

Lily's eyes widened. "A princess?" she gasped. "Where?"

"I told you," said Amber. "At the stables." She had been relating yesterday's events all through breakfast. But Lily, her younger sister, was like that. She didn't listen properly. Then, suddenly, she became interested and you had to tell her everything all over again.

"What's her name?" said Lily. "Can I see her?"

"No," said Amber.

Lily's bottom lip wobbled.

"Don't start," warned Amber, getting up.

"Mum, you tell her. I've got to go."

"Don't forget your invitations," said Mum.

Amber flew into the living-room to fetch them; her birthday sleepover was the following Saturday. She added them to her bag, along with her packed lunch.

"Who's coming?" said Lily.

"Molly and Lydia," replied Amber.

"And me," said Lily.

"Yes, and you," agreed Amber. Her little brother, Sam, was going to stay with Gran for the night and she'd hoped Lily would do the same. But Lily had decided otherwise.

"And the princess," said Lily.

Amber laughed. "No, silly! Not the princess."

"You can invite her if you like," said Mum. "Rana must be feeling lonely all that way from home."

"Ple–a–s–e," said Lily in that wheedling sing-songy voice that very often got her exactly what she wanted.

"I can't think now," said Amber, finding her riding hat. "I'll be late."

She wheeled her bicycle out of the shed, dumped her bag in the old-fashioned but very useful basket on the front and set off down the road.

It was all very well Mum having grand ideas about princesses. She didn't know what Rana was like. Amber could just imagine Rana's comments as she stepped through the back door into Sam's jumble of cars, farm animals and bits of puzzle. Even if she made it through to the living-room, she'd be met with Lily's dolls, colouring books and crayons occupying every available surface. Amber loved her home. She had no intention of giving Her Royal Highness the chance to pull it to pieces. If Rana was lonely, then she'd have to stay lonely.

But the thought niggled her.

Amber parked her bike next to the pony barn and hurried to the office. Parents and children were milling around outside the door, trying to get in to pay for "Tots and Beginners' Pony Day". Amber squeezed her way through and dumped her bag on the cupboard top with the other helpers' belongings. Carol was ticking people off the list as she took the money, and Jen was patiently explaining to two little boys that they couldn't both ride Misty – and why didn't one of them try Elf? She looked up as Amber came in.

"Lydia and Molly are tacking up," she said. "Rana's in the indoor arena with the little ones that are ready. She'll need some help."

Amber knew from experience that trying to keep a group of excited children – some of whom had never ridden before – calm was not easy. But when she reached the arena, there wasn't a murmur.

Rana had all the children marching past in a line and, as they drew level with her, each one stopped and said his or her name.

Then the whole process was repeated in the opposite direction; only this time, Rana said the child's name.

Sometimes, Rana couldn't remember – or *pretended* she couldn't. This was accompanied with hoots of joy. Hints were given: "It begins with..."

As Amber watched, a little girl with long blonde plaits approached. She stopped. "Don't tell me," Rana implored, her hand to her head in studied concentration. "I know: Emily Jane!"

Emily Jane nodded graciously and moved on.

But Charlotte, the next child, didn't move on when her name was guessed.

"Are you really a princess?" she demanded.

Rana smiled. "Yes."

"Do you live in a palace?"

"Yes, I do," said Rana.

Charlotte, satisfied, carried on to join the others.

Amber watched. Rana was completely at ease. She welcomed each new arrival and helped them to join in the game. By the time Molly and Lydia brought in the ponies, all the riders were there. Jen sorted them into groups, some to ride first, some to groom and some to muck out.

"What would you like to help with first?" Jen asked Rana.

"Whatever Amber's doing," replied Rana. Amber felt pleased to be chosen but couldn't help wondering why. She hadn't exactly been friendly towards the princess. She noticed Molly and Lydia exchanging glances. As they moved away with their group, Molly hissed, "Aren't you the honoured one?" and giggled with Lydia.

"We're mucking out to start with," said Amber. Rana nodded. She didn't seem disturbed by the news, though Amber doubted if she'd ever done it before.

The children loved it. Squeals of mirth

accompanied each carrying of droppings to the wheelbarrow, and if some happened to slip off the shovel on the way, the squeals became hysterical.

Grooming was a little quieter. Amber said she would give marks out of ten for the best-groomed pony, so the children brushed and currycombed with enthusiasm. Rana seemed to have no knowledge of either activity, but when their group came to ride, Rana helped them on, adjusted their stirrup leathers, tightened their girths and showed or reminded them how to hold the reins.

For the rest of the morning, Rana and Amber led ponies and their riders round and round the arena.

"Soon be our turn," Amber whispered near the end of the final lesson. "Jen's taking us to the proper cross-country course after lunch to practise for the competition."

At once, Rana's expression changed. One minute, she was relaxed and happy. The next, she wasn't. But Amber didn't have time to wonder about it. The children needed their "Special" rosettes, the ponies had to be untacked and Oscar had to be tacked up. By the time Amber was ready, Molly and Lydia had set off.

"Catch them up," said Jen. "Donna will meet us down there. I'll bring Rana in the car."

Amber rode along the path that led to the course. When she arrived, Jen and Rana were already there.

There was no sign of a pony for Rana.

"I think I'm too scared," said Molly, as Jen took them to look at the first jump.

It was a low fence set into a hedge. Jen assured them it was no bigger than the ones they were used to.

"But this is a real one!" said Molly.

They all laughed. That was the difference, of course. The jumps they knew were purpose-built and all arranged in one field.

These jumps were, for the most part, a natural feature of the countryside.

"Have a go anyway," encouraged Jen.

Amber went first. Oscar sailed over. Then she waited for the others. Molly joined her almost immediately, her face alight with success.

"Great!" said Amber. "Feather didn't hesitate!"

But Molly didn't respond. She turned to watch Lydia on Silver. Amber gave her attention to Oscar, who was fidgeting, wanting to get on.

The next jump was a stile with a step in front and behind. Again, Oscar took it in his stride. Jack was the only one who had trouble. His pony, Roger, kept stopping. "Leg on!" called Jen as he tried for the third time. Over they went.

"We haven't time to do the whole course today," said Jen. "We'll go across the field and finish with the water jump."

Rana doesn't look very happy, thought Amber, as they made their way. But then she wouldn't, with no pony to ride. And she'd worked hard all day, just like the rest of them. It wasn't fair.

Jen showed them the easy approach, down a sandy slope. "You only have to jump out of the water at novice level," she said.

Oscar couldn't wait. But Amber pulled him up. She jumped off and held out the reins to Rana. "Would you like to do this one?" she said. "I don't mind."

"No," said Rana at once, so sharply that Amber stared at her in surprise. She turned to Jen. "It's all right with me," said Jen.

Rana made no move. There was a moment's uncomfortable silence. Then she said, "I don't want to. And anyway, I don't ride." She walked away, fast, until she was running across the field, back to the car.

Amber lay in bed that night thinking about Rana's revelation and her sudden departure. If she didn't ride, what on earth was she doing spending the whole summer in a stables? It didn't make sense.

Rana was obviously used to horses. She hadn't been able to clean tack or groom. But when she'd been helping the little ones ride, she'd known exactly what she was doing.

Maybe Rana was *scared* to ride? Maybe she'd had a bad fall? That could put you right off.

When Amber arrived at the stables the next day, Rana met her and, at once, apologized. Amber listened in amazement as Rana said it had been very kind of her to offer the jump and she was sorry she'd been so rude – it was certainly nothing to do with Oscar.

"He's a lovely pony," she said, patting his neck.

Amber stopped brushing him. "He is, isn't he?" she agreed. Then, on an impulse, she said, "Would you like to come to my birthday sleepover? It's next Saturday at my house."

Rana's face flushed with pleasure. "I'd love to," she said. "But what is a sleepover?"

Amber explained and told her who would be there and how they'd probably have a midnight feast – and then she had to explain what that was. At each fresh piece of information, Rana got more and more excited.

"I'll have to ask," she said.

"Your parents?" said Amber.

"Actually, it's Pam," Rana replied. "She looks after me at the Hall."

"Like a maid?" said Amber, impressed.

"No." Rana laughed. "Although she does take care of my clothes and make me snacks if I'm hungry..."

"Oh," said Amber. "Like a mum!"

Rana's face clouded. "Not like *my* mother," she said.

There it was again. Just as you thought the conversation was going well, something nasty reared its head and Rana retreated into silence. But Amber hadn't time to worry about it now. She had to tack up Oscar ready to hack out with a group of pony-day riders. Mel, who was leading them, would expect her any minute.

When Amber returned an hour later, Rana was helping Jen set up a jumping course. Amber waved as she rode down the lane and Rana waved back. She looked happy, and Amber felt glad.

She decided to go and tell Molly about Rana coming to the sleepover.

"But you hardly know her," Molly objected. "Just because she's a princess."

"Don't be like that," said Amber. "You know you're my best friend."

"Doesn't look like it from where I'm standing," said Molly, and she went off to join Lydia.

All afternoon, Amber and Rana were kept busy helping with the scoring of the jumping course. Before each participant's round, Rana predicted the outcome.

"He'll knock the rail off the second part of the double," she said of a boy with bright red hair tearing round on Polka. And so he did.

"She'll clear everything," said Rana as a girl with freckles set off purposefully on Jester. And she did.

"How do you know?" said Amber, laughing.

"I'm guessing!" said Rana.

In the days that followed, Rana showed

no sign of wanting to get on a pony. She seemed to be settling down, though. She began to tackle the various tasks around the stables with a better grace than when she'd arrived.

One day, Donna turned up again. She didn't do much. Mostly, she pestered Rana with questions or relentlessly related the latest amazing exploits of Sparkle.

"You must come and see where he lives," enthused Donna. "Of course, I don't keep him here. He's at the livery yard at the Hall."

Rana paused in filling a hay-net.

"Where?" she said.

Donna, delighted at getting a response, told Rana again. "We could go now," she added. "It's not far."

"I'm working," said Rana abruptly.

"Quite right," said Jen, coming over. "I thought you'd come to help, Donna." She sent her off with Molly to tack up ponies and made sure she stayed with her for the rest of the day.

"It's not fair," said Molly as she and Amber cycled home. "I never see you. You're with Her Royal Highness the whole time. And she's even coming to your party!"

"That's where you're wrong," said Amber. "Rana's not coming."

When Rana had told her the following day that she wasn't allowed to accept Amber's kind invitation, Amber found she was really disappointed. But then there had followed an invitation from Rana. "Pam asked if you would like to come for a sleepover with me? At Merryfield Hall."

So Mum and Pam had met, and it was all arranged for the following weekend. Amber could hardly wait. She'd only been inside the Hall once, but she remembered the vast entrance, the tapestries on the walls and the enormous staircase.

She didn't tell Molly.

* * *

Amber's sleepover took place as planned. Mum prepared a delicious tea with sausages on sticks, strawberries and ice cream, and a wonderful birthday cake with chocolate buttercream that was decorated with three marzipan ponies: one lying down, one grazing and one balanced on its hindlegs, about to jump.

The midnight feast was a success too, and they managed not to wake Lily. But there was a distinct feeling of unease among the friends. Molly and Lydia chattered to each other incessantly. They whispered on into the night, keeping their voices low so that Amber couldn't hear what they were saying. For once, Mum didn't have to come in and tell them enough was enough.

Why was it so difficult to be friends with everybody? thought Amber. It wasn't her fault that Jen kept pairing her off with Rana. Anyway, Amber liked the princess now that she was getting to know her. But that didn't mean she no longer cared about Molly and Lydia.

Eventually, Amber turned over and pretended to go to sleep. This time next week, she'd be at Merryfield Hall.

The huge front door of Merryfield Hall Hotel stood wide open, letting in the hot August sunshine. Rana led Amber through the reception area and up the staircase, past a tapestry of a hunting scene which filled a whole wall.

Upstairs, they walked along a corridor lined with doors that had strange but interesting names: Campion Bell, Molly Pike, Zoffany.

"All the bedrooms are decorated differently," said Rana. "Wait till you see where we're sleeping!"

They turned the corner at the end of the

passage, and Rana opened the first door. “What do you think?”

Amber entered the room and felt she had stepped into the grounds of a stately home. Trees rich with summer growth were painted on every wall and they carried on up and over the ceiling into a soft blue sky. Flowers grew in the meadows. A stream wound its way into the distance. Iron railings edged a field close to them, beside which horses grazed. You could almost see them flicking their tails to ward off the flies. A pony gazed out at them.

“If you look carefully, you can see birds and animals everywhere,” said Rana, pointing out a kingfisher swooping below a stone bridge and a fox sneaking along a hedge.

Amber found a badger nosing out of its sett and an owl high in a tree. There were even ponies of different breeds embroidered on the bedspreads.

“It’s lovely,” breathed Amber. She had

never been in a room like it.

"Come on," said Rana. "Leave your things and we'll go and explore."

The afternoon raced by. Rana showed Amber the grounds: the maze where tiny hedges gave off a pungent smell as you wound your way in and out and around; the courtyards where they could play giant chess; and the lawns set up for croquet and pétanque. Rana took Amber along her favourite secret paths. There was a new delight round every corner: a stone seat set into the recess of a hedge; an entirely white flower garden; a kitchen garden with raspberry canes and gooseberry bushes; and a sundial that was over a hundred years old.

Once, Amber caught a glimpse of some buildings through the trees. She knew they were the old stables that had been turned into a livery yard, but she wouldn't get to see them. Rana was turning back towards the hotel.

"We've just got time for a swim before dinner," she said.

The pool was indoors, but today all its tall French windows stood open in the summer heat. After their swim, the girls sat on the patio sipping exotic fruit juice cocktails decorated with tiny sugar-dusted parasols. Amber asked if she could keep hers, and when Rana realized it was to take home for Lily, she gave Amber hers as well.

They talked about their families, their friends, their schools. But Amber noticed that not once did Rana bring up the subject of riding. Amber didn't like to either – if Rana had secrets she didn't want to reveal, that was fine.

They ate their meal in the main dining room, served by waiters with spotless white napkins over one arm. Amber had never eaten four courses before, but each one was delicious. She was even invited to have a second helping of raspberry meringue! As they dined, soft piano music drifted through from the drawing room.

Merryfield Hall was an amazing place, Amber decided as she fell asleep that night in the company of a host of animals.

Very early the following morning, Amber felt herself being shaken awake. Rana was already dressed.

"I want to show you something," she said.

"It had better be good!" grumbled Amber, pulling on her jeans and a top.

She followed Rana down the stairs and out of a side door. Quietly, they made their way into the gardens and through the trees. The earth smelt damp and fresh; there was a stillness in the air. When they came out into the open, Amber caught her breath. She knew where they were going.

They entered the livery yard through tall iron gates. Out of a stable opposite, a man led a young bay mare. She danced towards them, head held high, tail aloft.

"Hello, William," Rana greeted the man, before introducing Amber. "William's my instructor," she said. Amber murmured a reply but couldn't take her eyes off the mare.

"This is Emerald," said Rana, patting her neck. "She's—"

"Your precious jewel!" cried Amber. "Of course! She's an Arab, isn't she?" Amber had seen pictures of Arab ponies in her books. She recognized the small head set so neatly upon the neck, the intelligent eyes and the fineness of her body. "She's beautiful!"

"I'm glad you like her," said Rana. "I've been longing to tell you, but she's so valuable, I'm not supposed to tell people—"

William interrupted politely. "She's all ready for you," he prompted. Emerald was getting fidgety.

"Oh," said Rana. "Sorry. Would you like to stay, Amber?"

Amber nodded, her thoughts spinning. For the next hour, she watched. Not only could the princess ride; she rode well. She handled Emerald firmly but quietly. At first the mare jogged, spooked at nothing and bounded into canter. Gradually, Rana calmed her until they were moving in a lilting rhythm. Then, and only then, did William suggest trying some dressage shapes. He was a good teacher, but it was obvious that only the best would do. When that was achieved, he was generous in his praise.

"So you *do* ride!" said Amber the minute she joined Rana on the way back to the stable. "Really well!"

"My mother doesn't think so," said Rana. And out came the whole story.

Her mother had been an Olympic equestrian champion. None of Rana's older brothers and sisters, though proficient horsemen and women, had shown any inclination to follow in her footsteps. So she had pinned all her hopes on her youngest daughter.

"She spent a fortune buying Emerald and she made me practise for hours every day," said Rana. "But no matter how hard I tried, she was never satisfied. I lost my confidence completely. In the end, I gave up. What was the point? But I carried on riding Emerald in secret when my mother was away. Then she said I wasn't going to spend the whole summer doing nothing, so she sent me to work with Jen."

Amber found her head whirling again. "But why here? Why with Jen?"

Rana stared at her in surprise. "My parents own Merryfield Hall Hotel," she said. "Didn't you know?"

Amber shook her head. She'd had no idea.

"And one of the facilities they offer their guests is horse-riding..." continued Rana.

"...at Merryfield Hall Riding School!" said Amber.

"So my mother thought if I was working

there, I was bound to ride too, and that would get me back into it."

"Well, you could have!" cried Amber. "I'm sure Jen—"

"Oh, Jen was lovely," interrupted Rana. "It was me. I just couldn't face riding in front of anyone."

Amber smiled. "You've just ridden in front of me," she remarked.

"I know," Rana agreed. She finished rubbing Emerald down.

The two girls hung over the stable door, watching the mare tuck into her hay-net.

"My father sent her over on one condition," said Rana. "That William guards her day and night."

Amber was only half listening. "But now that Emerald *is* here," she said thoughtfully, "you could ride her in the show!"

"The One-Day Event?" said Rana. She pulled a face. "Guess who's presenting the prizes?"

Amber didn't need to guess. "But surely—"

"No," said Rana. "My mother would only be happy to present me with first prize. I couldn't do it. Definitely not."

But Amber had other ideas.

During the following week, Amber tried to persuade Rana to join in the free lessons at the stables. If she could get Rana to feel confident enough to ride in front of their group, maybe she'd change her mind about entering the show.

"You're entitled," said Amber. "You work just as hard as the rest of us."

"But I don't need to," Rana replied. "I've got William, haven't I?"

"They'd all be impressed," Amber told Rana on another occasion. "You're so good."

Rana laughed. "Thanks," she said, "but I prefer to ride on my own."

One day, Rana arrived at the stables with news.

"Guess who I saw this morning?"

Amber stopped mucking out. "Who?"

"I had the feeling someone was watching me," said Rana, "and the minute my lesson finished, Donna showed up. She couldn't take her eyes off Emerald. You can imagine the questions! How old was she? Was she an Arab? How much did she cost?"

Amber gasped. "Did you tell her?"

"Not exactly," said Rana. "But I think she'll work it out. Lots of people must know by now. After all, William sleeps in the stables."

"Well, if you can cope with Donna watching you, you'd be fine with us," said Amber.

To her surprise, Rana agreed. "William thinks it might be a good idea," she said.

Amber hid a smile.

That afternoon, when Rana arrived at the

lesson, not everyone was pleased to see her.

"I thought she didn't ride," hissed Molly as they warmed up.

"It's a long story," said Amber, trying to sit deep in the saddle.

"Well…?"

Amber hesitated. "I'm not sure how much Rana would want me—"

"Oh, forget it," snapped Molly, moving off.

The more Rana joined in the group lessons, the more relaxed she became. Almost everyone admired her skill, and they told her so. When, one day, Jack asked if she planned to take part in the One-Day Event, Amber knew what Rana's answer would be.

Preparations for the show began in earnest. Vast marquees were erected to house the prize vegetables, cakes, flowers and handicrafts. A funfair took shape in a large field behind the livery yard. Amber and Rana watched from an upstairs window at the Hall as dodgems, sideshows and roundabouts arrived and were set up. There was even a big wheel!

"I've always wanted to ride on one of those," said Rana. "There will be time, won't there?"

Amber assured her there would. "The fair stays at least a week after the One-Day Event," she said.

"But I fly home the day after," Rana replied. "We'll just have to fit it in."

Amber instantly felt anxious. Once she was at the showground, she would need to be with Oscar. She couldn't go charging off to the fair.

On the morning of the show, Amber was up early. By nine o'clock Oscar had been bathed, his socks scrubbed, his mane plaited, and his hooves oiled. Amber stood back to admire the result, and felt proud. Her first event, dressage, was at nine-thirty. At the last practice, Jen had been really pleased with her improvement. "Sit tall and enjoy it!" Jen had advised. Amber smiled to herself. She mounted and headed to the showground.

Rana was on first.

"I'm so nervous," she said when Amber arrived.

"Is your mother here?" asked Amber.

Rana pointed to a platform. "My parents just opened the show. They know I'm competing."

"You'll be fine," said Amber. She grinned. "Your mother will be really proud of you."

"That's what I'm worried about," said Rana as she rode into the arena.

Everyone got through the dressage test without any serious hitches. Emerald spooked at a tub of flowers on the way in but otherwise was her usual brilliant self. Oscar was on form, really listening to her, Amber thought as she began. Down the centre line they rode, straight and true, then a brisk trot round to A and into the Serpentine. Amber realized she was enjoying herself. She'd got the hang of where she needed to turn so that her loops were all the same size. And they were accurate at all the markers.

The next event was jumping. Both Oscar and Emerald achieved clear first rounds, and in the final round against the clock, Oscar flew and was clear. Only two other competitors had no faults. One was Emerald.

William came forward to take her as Rana rode out of the ring.

"Wasn't she amazing?" cried Rana as she dismounted.

William was quiet in his praise and offered congratulations to Amber too.

"Thanks," said Amber. "I'm really pleased with Oscar." She patted her pony's neck.

"William's off to see his brother," announced Rana. "He's in the vegetable tent with his prize marrows!"

But William wanted to take Emerald to the livery yard for a rest before the cross-country.

"I can do that," said Rana. "Amber'll come with me. There's bound to be somewhere to put Oscar too."

William protested, but at Rana's urging he decided to do as she suggested.

"No hurry," said Rana. "We've got over an hour."

The two girls set off down the drive on their ponies. The livery yard was deserted. Everyone was at the show. There was plenty of room for Oscar.

Once the ponies were settled, Amber took out her lunch from her rucksack. "Let's sit in the courtyard," she said, "in the sun."

But Rana had other ideas. "I'm going to the fair!"

Amber was shocked. "We can't!" she said. "You know we can't. What about Emerald?"

Rana looked uncomfortable. "We won't be long," she said. "She's quite safe."

Music blared from the fairground. "Come on!" said Rana.

From the top of the big wheel, you could see for miles. Over the livery yard to the cross-country course in one direction; over and beyond the Hall in another, to the arenas and marquees. In the far distance, a train made its way across the landscape, disappearing and reappearing between copses of trees. No sound of it reached the girls as they hovered gently at the wheel's topmost height, while passengers took their seats below.

"It's wonderful!" cried Rana. Amber had to agree. She just wished they could get a move on. The cross-country would be starting soon. As if in answer, the wheel began to turn, picking up speed until one moment they were plunging down into the noise of the barrel organs, sideshows and people, and the next swinging up, up above hedges, trees; round and round, the sights merging into a blur.

Just as Amber was beginning to feel the slightest bit giddy, the wheel began to slow and stopped. Behind them, passengers stepped out of their car. The wheel rose, taking Rana and Amber up, stage by stage, as people alighted below.

"We'll be the last to get out!" exulted Rana.

Amber looked at her watch anxiously. It was all taking far too long. The wheel rose again. Amber sat on the edge of her seat, more from worry than because she wanted to see, but then something caught her eye. A horsebox was reversing into the livery yard. The back was lowered. When the wheel stopped again, Amber leant out to see what was going on. A pony was being led out of the stables. It danced along, head held high, tail aloft. With only a little persuasion, the beautiful bay stepped delicately up the ramp into the box.

Amber found her voice. "Rana! Someone's stealing Emerald!"

The wheel turned agonizingly slowly, it seemed to Amber, as they began their descent. Rana clutched the steel safety bar. "Come on! Come on!" she kept saying.

As soon as the girls were released from their cage, they ran, weaving through the crowds of people and at last emerging through trees at the livery yard.

"They'll be gone. I know they will," cried Rana.

But the horsebox was still there, its engine spluttering … and dying. Rana ran to the driver's door and wrenched it open.

"Get out!" she screamed.

The driver reached over and pulled the door from her, slamming it shut. He tried the engine again. It spluttered, this time into life. Rana jumped out of the way as it lurched forward.

Amber was standing in the gateway, directly in the horsebox's path.

"No!" screamed Rana.

But Amber stood her ground. The horse-box had to stop. Surely even thieves would not run her down.

The horsebox kept coming. Amber could see the two men in the cab shouting at her to get out of the way. Then she felt herself grabbed and hauled to one side. The horse-box swerved past. She picked herself up.

"You shouldn't have done that!" she yelled at Rana. "They'd have stopped."

Rana was crying.

Amber ran after the horsebox, watching to see which way it would turn when it reached the lane. As she raced back, she was aware of a voice calling to her. But she kept going. There was no time to lose.

"Come on!" she said to Rana. "Help me tack up Oscar. I've got an idea."

Rana listened, her face white.

Amber led Oscar into the yard. Molly was there on Feather. "What's going on?" she cried. "I'd just brought Feather out to warm him up before the cross-country when I saw you. I did shout..."

"Emerald's been stolen," said Rana.

Amber ignored Molly. She spoke to Rana. "Go for help," she said. "Tell someone what's happened."

"I can't," whispered Rana. "My mother'll kill me. I'm coming with you."

"That's silly," said Amber, mounting. "You won't be able to keep up on foot. Please, Rana."

"Take Feather," said Molly, jumping off. "I'll go for help."

Quickly, Amber told Molly her plan. Then

she urged Oscar into a brisk trot down the path and out onto the cross-country course. If they followed it over the fields, there was a chance they could get ahead of the horse-box and stop it, or at least get its registration number.

Amber pushed Oscar forward into a fast canter. Almost before she realized it, they were over the first jump and heading for the stile, Rana and Feather close behind. Over that too and making for the old quarry.

"Watch out for the drop!" Amber yelled as they approached it. The quarry was overgrown now, full of trees and plants, but the jump into it entailed a steep slope.

Rana shouted back: "I remember!"

Oscar didn't hesitate. Amber landed safely and, once down on level ground, she glanced back to see if Rana was with her. Feather flew over. Amber had never seen Feather so responsive. Rana knew what she was doing.

Then they were jumping out of the quarry and galloping uphill. Amber leant forward in the saddle and urged Oscar on. He needed no second telling. His stride lengthened as he surged ahead.

At the top of the hill, the course entered a small copse of pine. Amber steadied Oscar as they followed the twisty path. There was a fallen tree trunk to leap at the end. Then they were out into the open again and taking the downhill run as fast as they dared. At the bottom, there was a gap in the hedge with a ditch.

Oscar soared over. After that, the course led back to the Hall, but Amber turned Oscar the opposite way towards an open gate at the edge of the field. In the lane she pulled up, breathless, scanning it in both directions.

They were too late.

To the left, in the distance, was the horsebox.

Amber's instinct was to charge after it, but she knew it was hopeless. They'd never catch it.

Then she saw something: red lights; barriers swinging down. The level crossing.

A train was coming!

That would stop the horsebox.

Amber spurred Oscar into action. Rana followed. At a fast trot, they sped down the lane.

Amber sang out loud: "We're nearly there!" They were getting closer and closer.

But they weren't close enough.

The train flashed past. The barriers rose. The horsebox moved forward.

Amber wanted to scream in her disappointment.

But then a piercing screeching filled the air.

On the other side of the crossing, their sirens blaring, two police cars brought the horsebox to a standstill.

* * *

The farewell party for Rana took place at Merryfield Hall at noon the following day. Guests assembled in the drawing room and spilled out onto the sunshine-filled courtyard.

Molly was there, and Lydia and Jack. Jen and Carol were there too, along with Rana's parents. Everyone was talking about the happenings of the previous day. The thieves had been caught: two local men with an eye to easy money. Emerald had been freed from the horsebox and they'd arrived back in time to take part in the cross-country. Despite their exhausting experience, Rana rode Emerald to victory, not only in the field event but in the competition itself. Rana's mother had been delighted to present her daughter with first prize.

"I just wish William didn't blame himself," Rana told Amber. "I know it was all my fault. I've explained everything to my mother. We had a long talk, and she says William can teach me from now on, if I'm serious about riding."

"So you're all set for the Olympics!" said Amber.

Rana's mother came towards them. She congratulated Amber on taking second place at the show and then sent Rana off to fetch drinks.

"You've been such a good friend to my daughter," she said. "I can't thank you enough for helping her regain her confidence. And for what you did yesterday. You were very brave to give chase."

Amber smiled. "Come and meet Molly," she said. "We couldn't have done it without her. It was Molly who called the police."

At two o'clock, all the guests went out to the helipad to see Rana and her parents depart. Amber stood and waved until the helicopter was a speck in the distance. "I'll miss you," Rana had whispered just before she boarded, and Amber knew she'd miss the princess too.

As everyone turned to go back to the Hall, Molly and Lydia appeared, one on each side of Amber. "We're going to the fair," they said. "Want to come?"

It's Pony Day at Merryfield Hall Riding School and, for the first time ever, Dad has promised to come and watch Amber jump. Everything will be perfect ... as long as Amber gets to ride her favourite pony, Beany. But Donna wants to ride Beany too – and, as the jumping competition gets closer, it looks like she'll go to any lengths to get her own way!

By June Crebbin

It's the first day of Pony Camp at Merryfield Hall Riding School. Five whole days of riding! Amber has been looking forward to it for months. But that evening, Amber sees Oscar the pony being bullied by some boys and she hatches a plan to save him…

Amber is excited to be going pony-trekking in Wales. Three days of trail riding across hills and along beaches – even wild camping! But Donna isn't happy and just wants to cause trouble. When the expedition faces disaster, Amber has to do some quick thinking!

It's the biggest adventure of Rollo's life!

William, Duke of Normandy, has invaded England to conquer King Harold and take his crown. Can Rollo, his pageboy, help William win the battle and become King of England?

**If you've enjoyed reading this book, look out for...**

**Short novels for fluent readers**